Mom ~

I'm grateful for your humor, your advice, and your support. You raised me to be generous, persistent, and forgiving – and it has served me well. Thank you for loving me so completely.

www.mascotbooks.com

There's Something Pokey in My Shoe

©2017 Kelly Jean Lietaert. All Rights Reserved. No part of this publication may be reproduced, stored in a retrieval system or transmitted in any form by any means electronic, mechanical, or photocopying, recording or otherwise without the permission of the author.

For more information, please contact:
Mascot Books
560 Herndon Parkway #120
Herndon, VA 20170
info@mascotbooks.com

Library of Congress Control Number: 2017906109

CPSIA Code: PBANG0717A
ISBN-13: 978-1-68401-398-2

Printed in the United States

THERE'S SOMETHING POKEY IN MY SHOE

KELLY JEAN LIETAERT

Stay positive..

Kelly Jean Lietaert

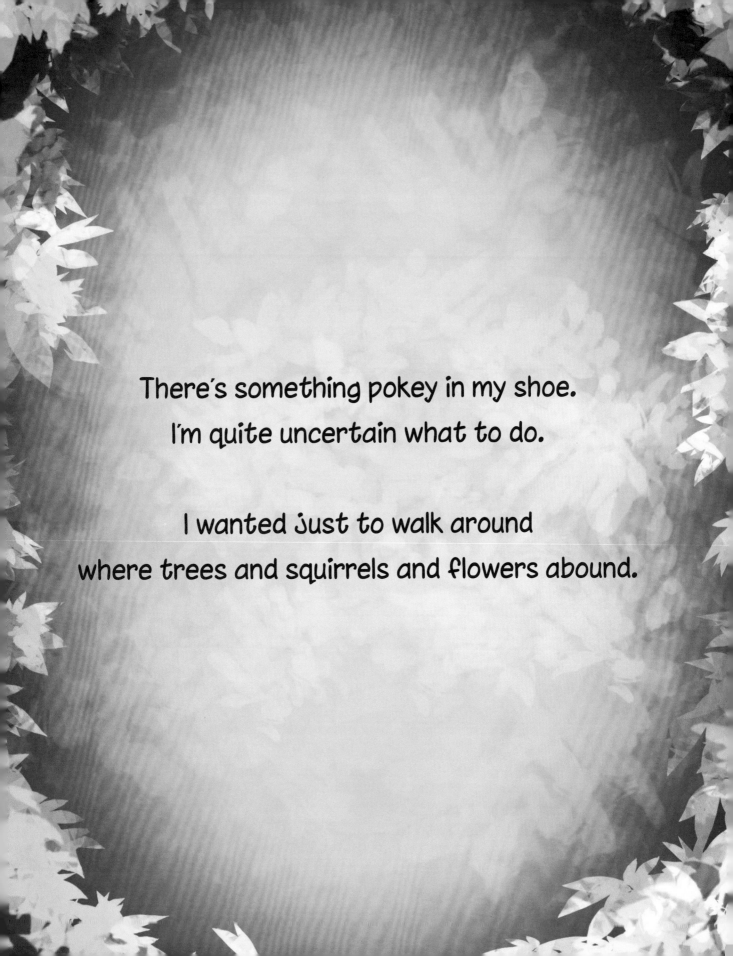

There's something pokey in my shoe.
I'm quite uncertain what to do.

I wanted just to walk around
where trees and squirrels and flowers abound.

I wiggle my toes and move my heel.
My sister says, "It's no big deal!"

Our family is going to ride our bikes.
And after that we'll take a hike.

My feet will do a lot of the work,
pushing the pedals and stomping the dirt.

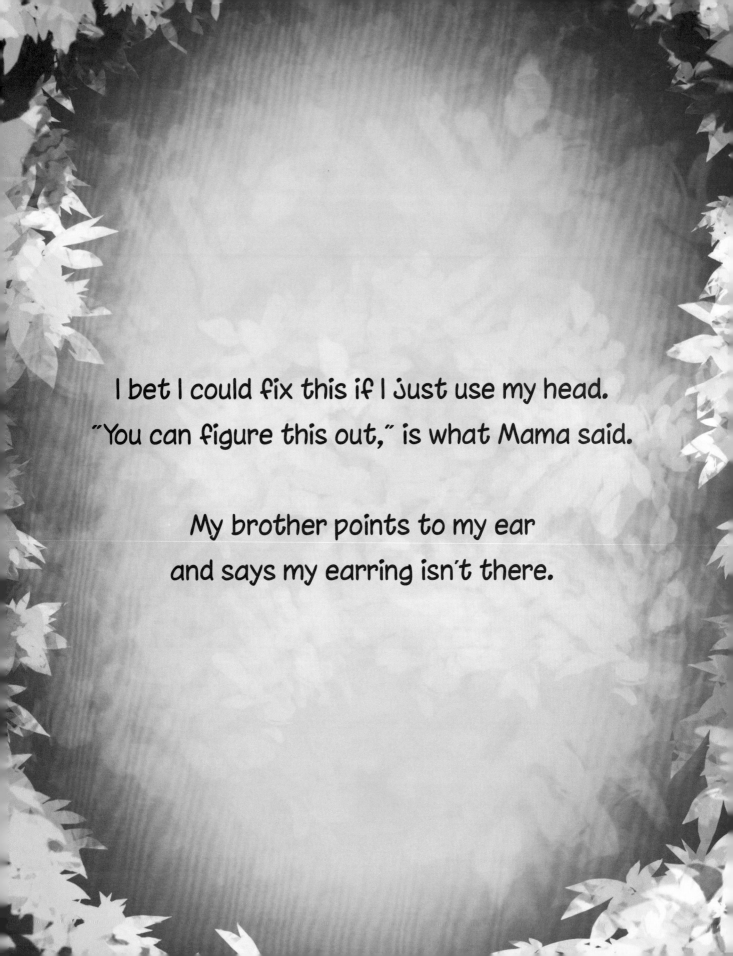

I bet I could fix this if I just use my head.
"You can figure this out," is what Mama said.

My brother points to my ear
and says my earring isn't there.

Oh geez! I can't believe this day!
When will things start to go my way?

I want to run and jump and play.
No pokey thing will ruin my day!

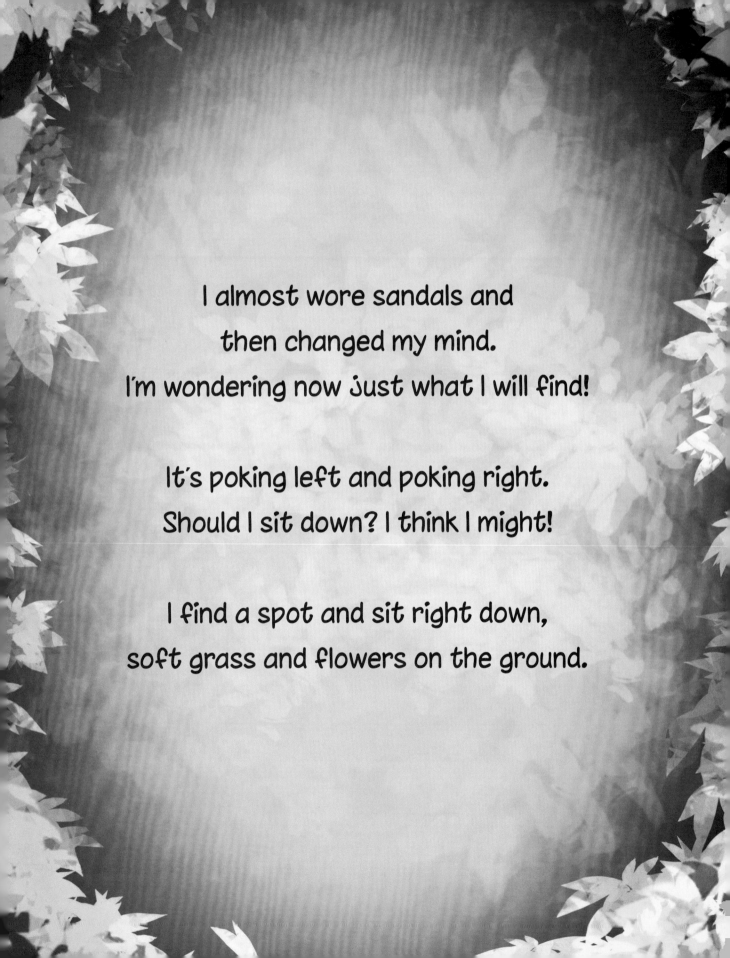

I almost wore sandals and
then changed my mind.
I'm wondering now just what I will find!

It's poking left and poking right.
Should I sit down? I think I might!

I find a spot and sit right down,
soft grass and flowers on the ground.

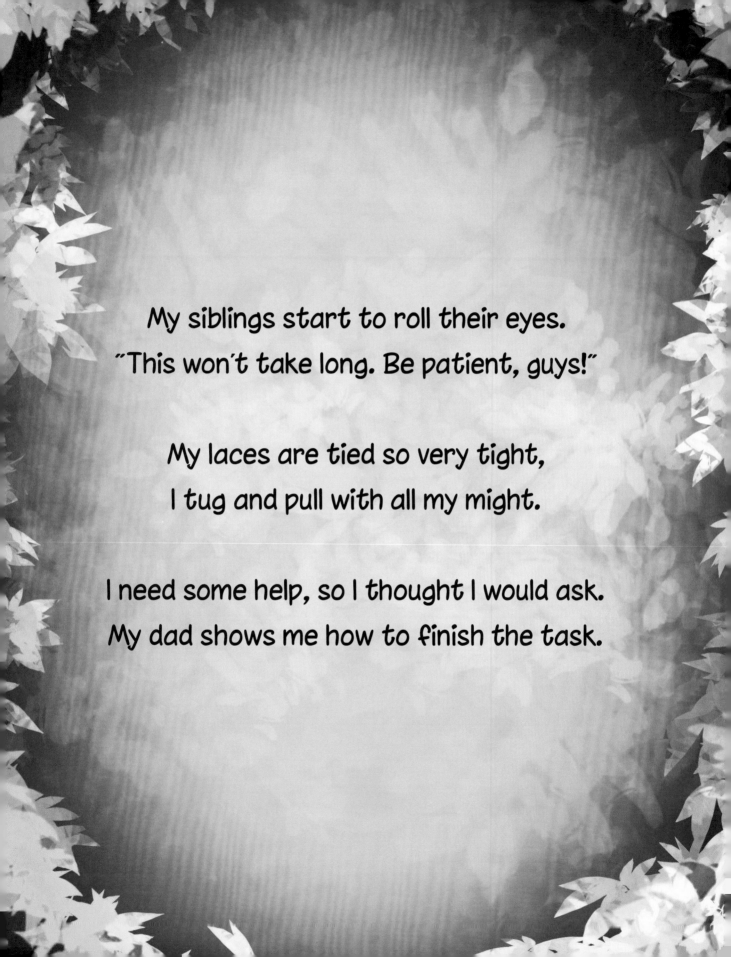

My siblings start to roll their eyes.
"This won't take long. Be patient, guys!"

My laces are tied so very tight,
I tug and pull with all my might.

I need some help, so I thought I would ask.
My dad shows me how to finish the task.

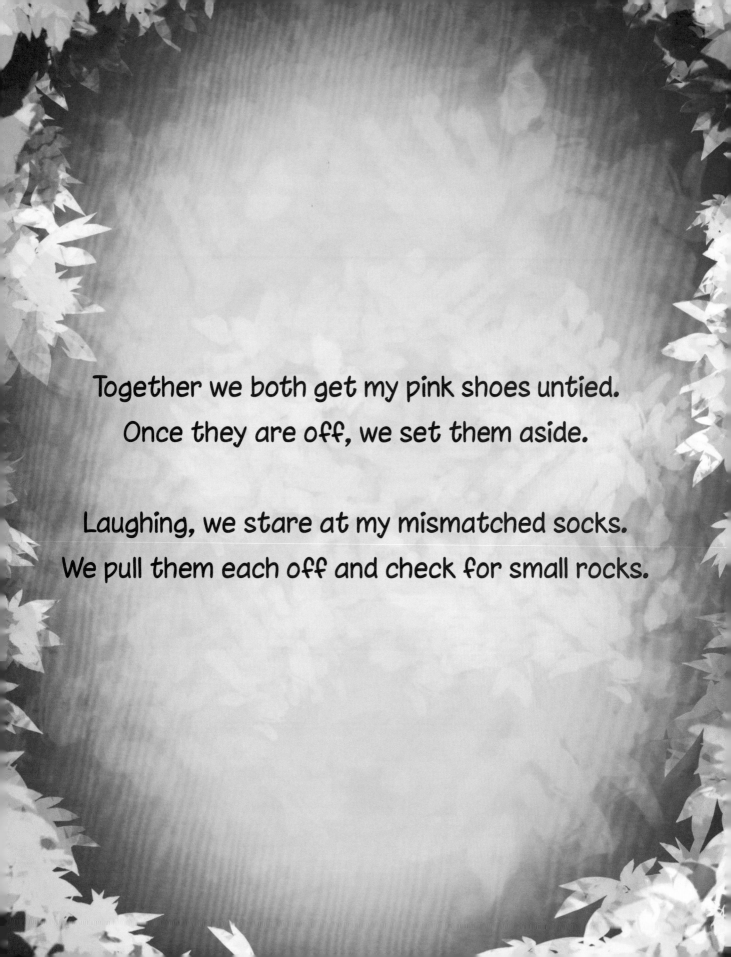

Together we both get my pink shoes untied.
Once they are off, we set them aside.

Laughing, we stare at my mismatched socks.
We pull them each off and check for small rocks.

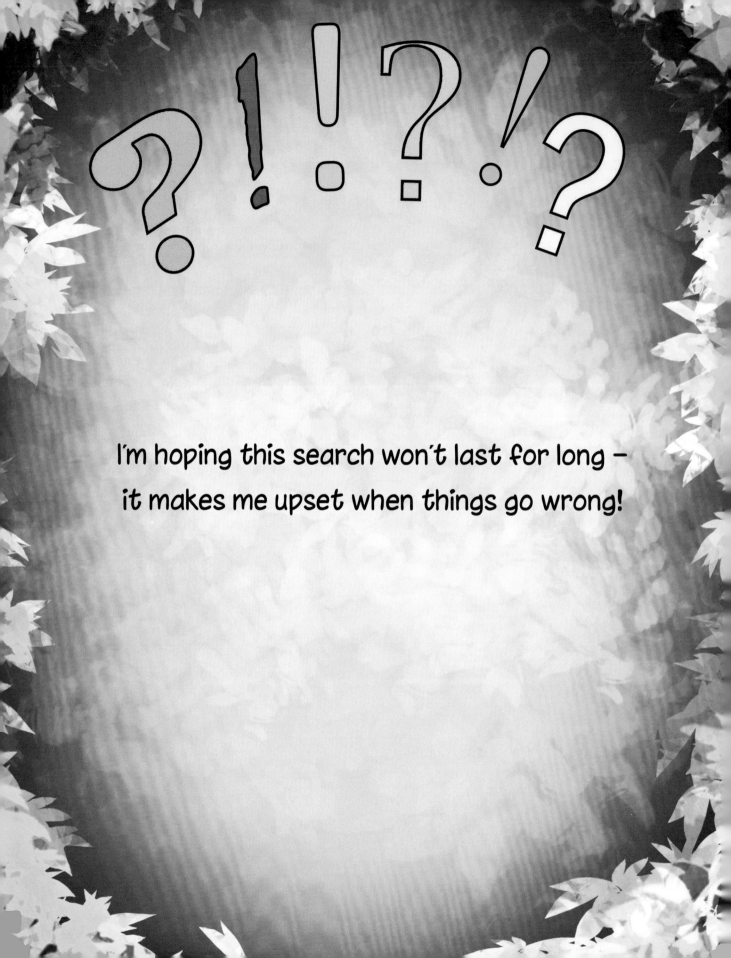

I'm hoping this search won't last for long –
it makes me upset when things go wrong!

But wait! What is that in my shoe?
It's sparkly, blue, and pokey too!

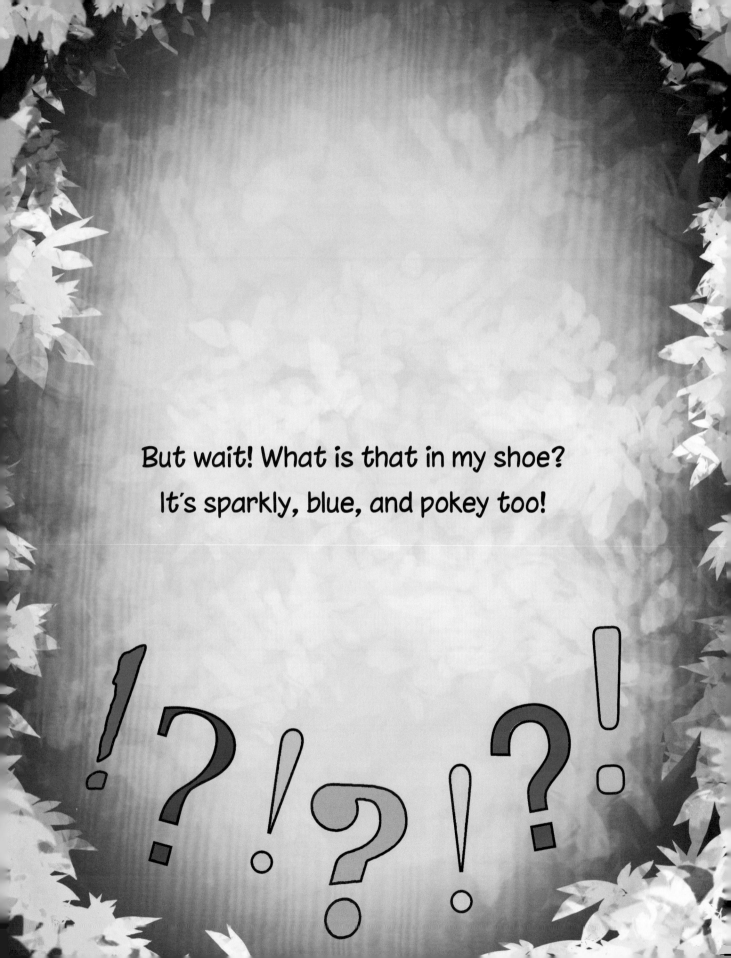

Right there, on the side, by my baby toe!
No wonder it hurts, it had no place to go!

My earring! We found it! We just saved the day!
Now we can laugh and hike and play.

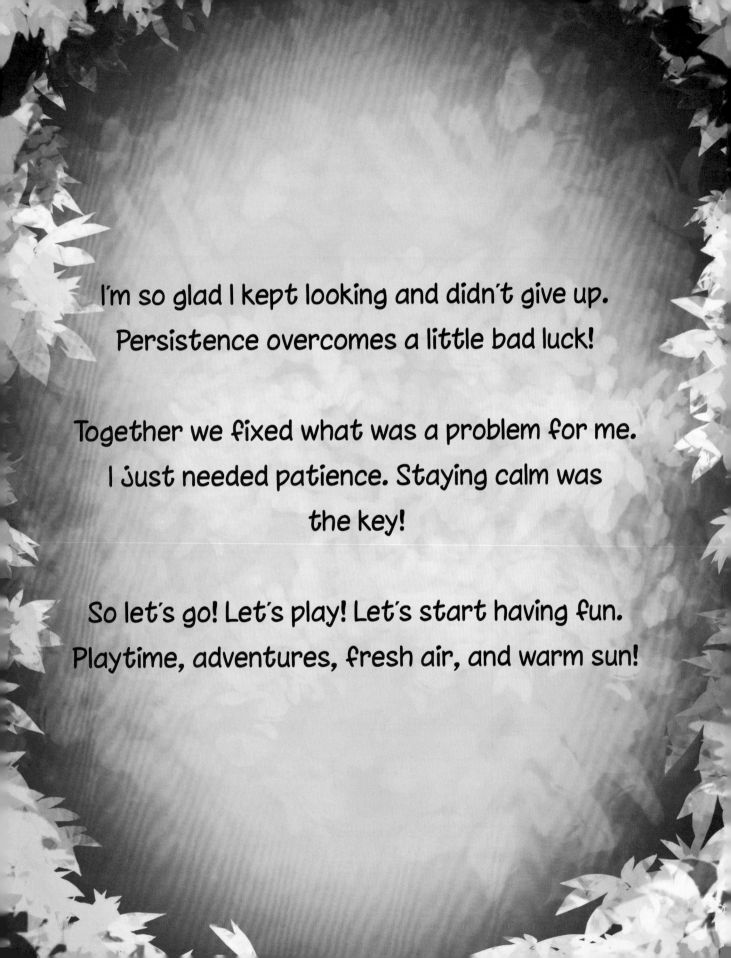

I'm so glad I kept looking and didn't give up.
Persistence overcomes a little bad luck!

Together we fixed what was a problem for me.
I just needed patience. Staying calm was
the key!

So let's go! Let's play! Let's start having fun.
Playtime, adventures, fresh air, and warm sun!

Word Search

Can you find all the words?

```
P A S T H V G N B R J E
L J Z F R Q H P B Z C V
E K K S A Q A T W N P Y
H F N E X M S W E H O K
H U G R E V I I Y T K N
F P N U U P T L D T E U
P G G T V A Z V Y N Y G
H Q H N P L I Z Z I E S
S Z N E E A O S V V H E
U Y P V E K I H W O X G
E X X D H A I P E G D C
A I Y A U T D B A J S H
```

ADVENTURES	HELP	POKEY
BIKE	HIKE	SHOE
FAMILY	LIZZIE	
FUN	PATIENCE	

Let's Talk!

1. How do you react when things go wrong?
2. What are your favorite outside activities? If you can't go outside, what do you like to do?
3. Why was it helpful that Lizzie didn't become upset?
4. How could you help someone if they are having trouble?
5. Who do you go to when you need help?
6. It's easy to give up. When have you had to work extra hard to solve a problem?

ANSWERS

1. shoe 2. hike 3. bike 4. pokey 5. family

6. patience 7. adventures 8. Lizzie 9. fun 10. help

Word Scramble

Can you unscramble these words?

1. heso _____

2. kieh _____

3. ebik _____

4. kepoy _____

5. layimf _____

6. cieepnta _____

7. nedvarutes _____

8. ileziz _____

9. nuf _____

10. pehl _____

About the Author

New author Kelly Lietaert has an early childhood degree and has always loved writing. She enjoys strong coffee, loud music, and laughing with her family. Married for 21 years to her Prince Charming, you can find her in Michigan caring for their four kids and two lazy cats.